For my boy with the Bedhead
—M. P.

For John, Michael, and Jason
—J. E. D.

First Aladdin Paperbacks edition August 2003

Text copyright © 2000 by Margie Palatini
Illustrations copyright © 2000 by Jack E. Davis

ALADDIN PAPERBACKS
An imprint of Simon & Schuster Children's Publishing Division
1230 Avenue of the Americas
New York, NY 10020

Also available in a Simon & Schuster Books for Younger Readers hardcover edition.
Designed by Lily Malcom and Jennifer Reyes
The text of this book was set in 18-point Kosmik.
The illustrations were rendered in colored pencil, acrylic, dye, and ink.

Manufactured in China
20 19

The Library of Congress has cataloged the hardcover edition as follows:
Palatini, Margie.
Bedhead / by Margie Palatini ; illustrated by Jack E. Davis
    p.    cm.
Summary: After many unsuccessful attempts to control his unruly hair one morning,
Oliver and his family think that they have solved the problem—until he gets to school
and finds that it is school picture day.
ISBN 978-0-689-82397-8 (hc)
[1. Hair—Fiction.] I. Davis, Jack E., ill. II. Title.
PZ7.P1755Bg 2000
[Fic]—dc21
98-31660
ISBN 978-0-689-86002-7 (Aladdin pbk.)
0815 SCP

# BEDHEAD

by Margie Palatini

•

illustrated by Jack E. Davis

Aladdin Paperbacks
New York    London    Toronto    Sydney    Singapore

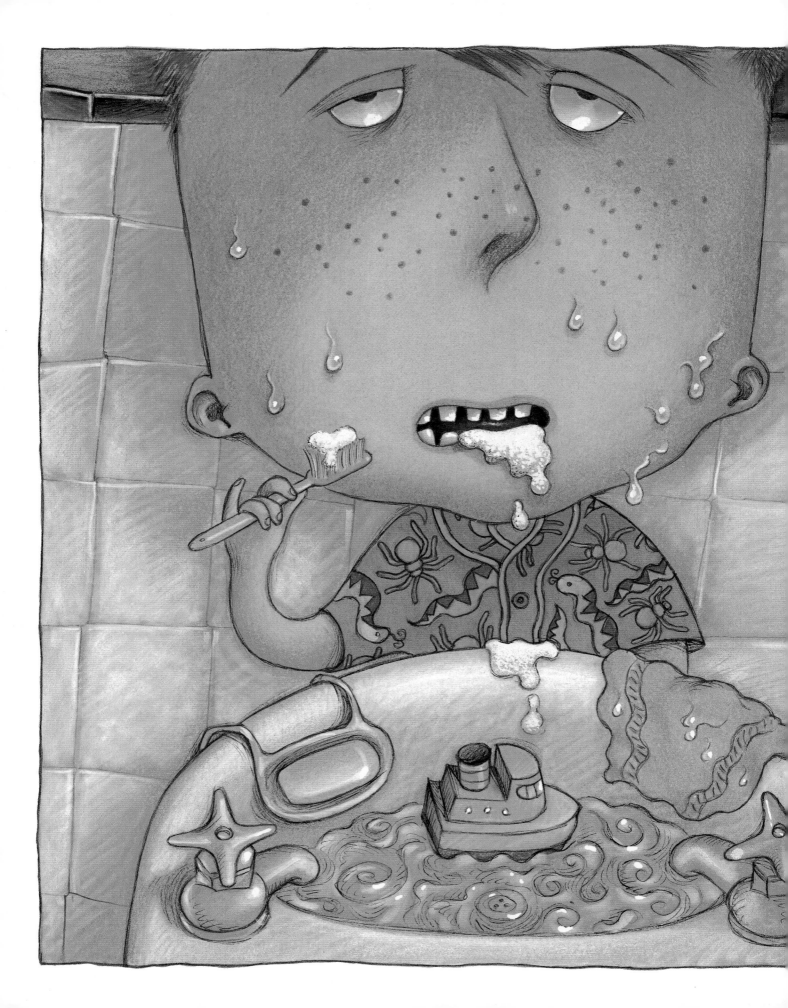

**Shuffle-shlump. Shuffle-shlump. Shuffle-shlump,**

shlumped bleary-eyed Oliver out of bed, down the hall, and into the bathroom.

He yawned.

He yanked.

Splashed some water.

Swished some mouthwash.

Gave his front teeth a passable brushing.

And then . . .

In a gunkless corner of the soapy silver soap dish . . . in a fogless smidgen of his father's foggy shaving mirror . . . right there on the hot water faucet, for heaven's sake . . . he saw it!

It was **BIG.**

It was **BAD.**

It was . . .

# BEDHEAD!

Oliver's hair was out of control.

*Way* out of control.

There was hair going this way. Hair going that way. Hair going up. Down. Around and around. And there was one teeny tiny clump of hair way at the back of his head that looked just like a cat's coughed-up fur ball.

"aaaaAAAAAAHHHHHHHhhhhhhhhhhhh!"

Oliver's scream shook. It rattled. It rolled all the way down the stairs and into the kitchen where Froot Loops went flying. Milk was spilled, spit, and sputtered. And two toast toasties did triple back flips onto the breakfast table.

"Oliver? Oliver? OLIVER!" shouted Mom, Dad, and Emily as they ran up the stairs and headed for the bathroom door.

Mom leaned close to the door. Closer. Closer. That's right—
*even* closer.

"Is everything all right, Oliver?" she whispered in her calmest
calm Mom voice. "Come now, dear. Open the door and let us in."

No sound from Oliver. Not a whimper. Not a peep.

"Please?" said Mom. "Pretty please? . . . Pretty, pretty, pretty
please? . . ."

The doorknob s l o w l y turned.

Mom smiled at Dad. She gave a wink to Emily. "There you
go," she said, taking a step into the bathroom. "Nothing can
be that . . .

BaaaaaaAAAddddddd!"

Wrong. It was that bad.

"Yes sir, no doubt about it," said Dad, surveying the hairy situation from sinkside. "Oliver, my boy, you're having one bad hair day."

"Major," said Mom.

"Total," agreed Emily.

"Maybe if we just push it this way," Mom said, giving it a try.

BOING.

"Been there. Done that," moaned Oliver.
"Perhaps if we just pull it that way," said Dad.
BOING.

"Been there. Done that," groaned Oliver.
"I could curl it!" offered Emily, ready to roll.
Oliver stared a steely stare at his sister. "I don't think so."
"Oh, then we'll just wet it!" said Mom.
"Yes! Let's just wet it!" they all agreed.

So—they watered Oliver.

They splished him. And splashed him. Gave him a good soak and dunk.

"Aaah," they said, sighing a confident, job-well-done sigh.

Oliver's bedhead was now one dripping wethead.

And then . . .

It dried.

B-B-B-Boing! B-BOING! Bink-Bink B-B-B-BOING!

Hair started going this way. Hair started going that way. Then up. Down. Around and around. And there was now a *bigger* clump of hair way at the back of his head that looked just like a cat's coughed-up fur ball.

"I say we spray!" shouted Dad, taking aim with a squirt.

"Yes! Spray! Spray!" cried out Mom and Emily.

"So spray already!" sputtered Oliver.

So they spritzed him and sprayed him. And they gooped, glopped, and moussed him. They even hair-pinned him flat in five places for good measure.

"Aaah," they said, sighing a confident, job-well-done sigh.

Oliver's bedhead was now one slick gelhead.

And then . . .

Pins went **f-f-f-flying!**

B-B-B-Boing! B-Boing! Bing-Bing B-B-B-Boing!

Hair started going this way. Hair started going that way. Then up. Down. Around and around. And there was now an *even bigger* clump of hair way at the back of his head that looked just like a cat's coughed-up fur ball.

Oliver wondered, "Maybe if I just sort of . . . kind of . . . you know, brushed it a bit?"

"No! No!" the three shouted, seeing the boy with bristles poised. "Whatever you do, no, no . . . **No Brush!**"

Too late.

Oooh yes. The brush got stuck. Not stuck in the hair going this way or that. Not stuck in the hair going up and down. Not even stuck in the hair going around and around. But stuck, yes, very, very, very stuck in the clump way at the back of his head that looked just like a cat's coughed-up fur ball.

Mom gave it a yank.

"E-Oooow!"

Dad gave it a pull.

"oOO-Ouch!"

And Emily gave it one good long tug.

"Y-Y-Y-Yike!"

"Well," said Mom without a bit of a doubt. "That brush is stuck, all right."

"Definitely stuck," decided Dad.

"A done deal," declared Emily.

Then, just when they all were about to give up hope, Oliver saw the answer right there on the wall!

EEEEEEEOOWW

"That's it!" he pointed. "THE HAT! **THE HAT!**
**GO GET THAT HAT!**"

So without one more thought of a spritz,
spray, or dunk, they all helped Oliver squish,
smoosh, and cram every bit of bedhead, stuck
brush and all, into his faithful, old, battered,
but true-blue baseball cap.

Well, almost. Eh. Good enough.

And with a kiss and a wave, Oliver headed off
to school.

Everything was fine. Everything was dandy.
And then . . .

Mary Margaret, who sat in the third row, four seats down, one desk across from Oliver in Mrs. Oppenheimer's class at Biddlemeyer Elementary, looked over to him and said, "You can't wear that hat."

Oliver looked over to Mary Margaret. "Can too."

"Can not."

"And just, why not?" demanded Oliver, holding tightly on to his hat.

Mary Margaret grinned. "Because it's picture day."

"P-P-PICTURE DAY?" stuttered Oliver.

"PICTURE DAY!" sang out Mrs. Oppenheimer, standing in front of the class. "Everyone line up for our class picture! Backs straight. Faces front. Smiles wide. And . . . and . . . HATS OFF!"

"Uh-oh," said Oliver. "Hats off?"

"We're waiting, Oliver!" said Mrs. Oppenheimer as everyone took their places.

"We're waiting, Oliver!" said Mary Margaret.

"We're waiting, Oliver!" said everyone else.

"Hey, kid," said the man behind the camera. "Yeah, you with the lumpy-looking head. Off with that hat!"

Oliver hemmed. He hawed. But he knew he had had it. He lifted the brim and slowly took off his faithful, old, battered, but true-blue baseball cap.

He held his breath. He closed his eyes. And he waited. He waited some more.

Nothing. Zero. Zilch. Nada.

He opened his eyes and looked up.

There was no hair going this way. No hair going that way. No hair going up. Down. Not even around and around. And nobody could see the brush stuck in the clump of hair way at the back of his head that looked like a cat's coughed-up fur ball.

"Aaah," said Oliver, sighing a confident, job-well-done sigh.

"Ready, everyone?" sang out Mrs. O. "Big smiles, and say 'Cheese' on the count of three."

"ONE!" she said. "TWO!" she said.

And then ... then ... T H E N ...

b-b-b-B-B . . . BOING! Boing! Bing-Bing B-B-B-BOING! BOING! Boing! B-B-B-BOING!

Hair started going this way. Hair started going that way. Hair started going up. Down. Around and around. And the brush that was stuck in the clump of hair way at the back of his head that looked just like a cat's coughed-up fur ball let loose and boinged Mary Margaret on top of her head and boomeranged right into Mrs. Oppenheimer's nose.

"THREE?" said the boinked Mrs. O just as she and everyone else at Biddlemeyer Elementary got a look at Oliver and his bedhead.

"aaaaaAAAAAAHHHHHHHHHHhhhhhhh—Geeez!"

Click.

"Got it!" said the photographer.

MRS. OPPENHEIMER'S CLASS: (FRONT ROW)
DANIEL, GEOFFREY, SARAH, JESSICA, MICHAEL,
MRS. OPPENHEIMER. (MIDDLE ROW) KATHRYN,

BEN, TIM, MARY MARGARET, EMMA. (BACK ROW)
ROBERT, ALLISON, ANDREW, ERIN, STEVEN,
OLIVER . . . AND OF COURSE, OLIVER'S BEDHEAD.